Richard Scarry's
DAY OF ADVENTURES

RANDOM HOUSE 🏠 NEW YORK

Richard Scarry's A Day at the Airport © 2001 by Richard Scarry Corporation. *Richard Scarry's A Day at the Fire Station* © 2003 by Richard Scarry Corporation. All rights reserved. Published in the United States by Random House Children's Books, a division of Random House, Inc., 1745 Broadway, New York, NY 10019.

These works were originally published separately in the United States by Random House Children's Books as *Richard Scarry's A Day at the Airport*, in 2001, and as *Richard Scarry's A Day at the Fire Station*, in 2003.

Visit us on the Web!
randomhouse.com/kids

Educators and librarians, for a variety of teaching tools, visit us at
RHTeachersLibrarians.com

978-0-375-97298-0

Printed in the United States of America   10 9 8 7 6 5 4 3 2 1

Richard Scarry's
A Day at the Airport

Father Cat wants to take Huckle,
Sally, and Lowly out sailing this afternoon.
Plink! Plop! Plink!
Uh-oh, Father Cat, it's starting to rain.

He puts the
top up on the car.

"There's nothing to do but to go back home."

What a
disappointment.

Father Cat stops at Scotty's Filling Station for gasoline.
"Fill 'er up, please, Scotty!" Father Cat says.
Just then, Rudolf Von Flugel drives up in his airplane-car.
"Good afternoon, Father Cat!" says Rudolf. "Are you going sailing?"

"No, we're going home, Rudolf," Father Cat says sadly.
"The children will have to play inside today."

"Hmm," says Rudolf. "Why don't they come with me? I'm
going to the airport. There's lots to see there, even when it rains!"

"Wow! Can we, Dad?" Huckle asks.

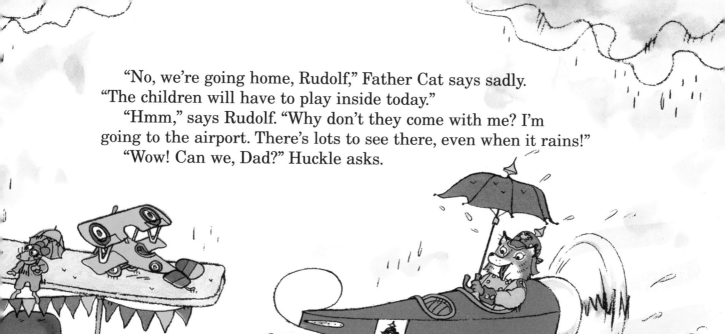

Father Cat thinks it is a great idea.
He helps place the children in Rudolf's
airplane-car.

"Don't worry, Father Cat.
I'll bring the children home
dry as baked apple strudel!"
says Rudolf.

And off they go!
Brruumm!

radar

runway

pier

catering truck

control tower

catering kitchen

snowplow

airport bus

They arrive at the airport in no time.

wind sock

runway lights

hangar

a tractor towing a plane

restaurant

departure terminal

parking garage

ARRIVALS DEPARTURES

arrivals

taxis

My, what a busy place it is!

check-in counters

TO PARIS ⬇

TO NEW YORK ⬇

TO VENICE ⬇

conveyor belt

scale

luggage cart

"Here we are!" Rudolf says, driving into the departure terminal.

CLOSED ✕

TO WORKVILLE ⬇

TO THE GATES ➡

Mind your head!!

luggage tag

DEPARTURES	TIME	GATE
PARIS	3:30	2
WORK VILLE	4:00	1
VENICE	4:02	3
NEW YORK	5:15	1
LONDON	5:30	3
TOKYO	6:00	2

lots of luggage

porter

"These are the check-in counters. Passengers show their tickets here, and also have their baggage weighed and tagged with its destination," Rudolf explains. "Each passenger receives a boarding pass to enter the plane at the gate."

check-in hostess

ticket

boarding pass

"The airport terminal is like a small Busytown," says Rudolf. "There are shops that sell books, toys, and flowers. And there's a police station, a post office, and a first-aid center, too!"

"Is there a bathroom, Mr. Von Flugel?" Sally asks.

While they wait for Sally, Lowly asks if there is also a restaurant at the airport. "Travel always makes me thirsty!" he laughs.

As soon as Sally returns, Rudolf drives up the escalator to the restaurant.

restaurant

catering truck

boarding gate

WORKVILLE

passenger bus

kerosene fuel is pumped into tanks in the wings

baggage train

hose

fire extinguisher

cleaning truck

paper to recycle

bottles to recycle

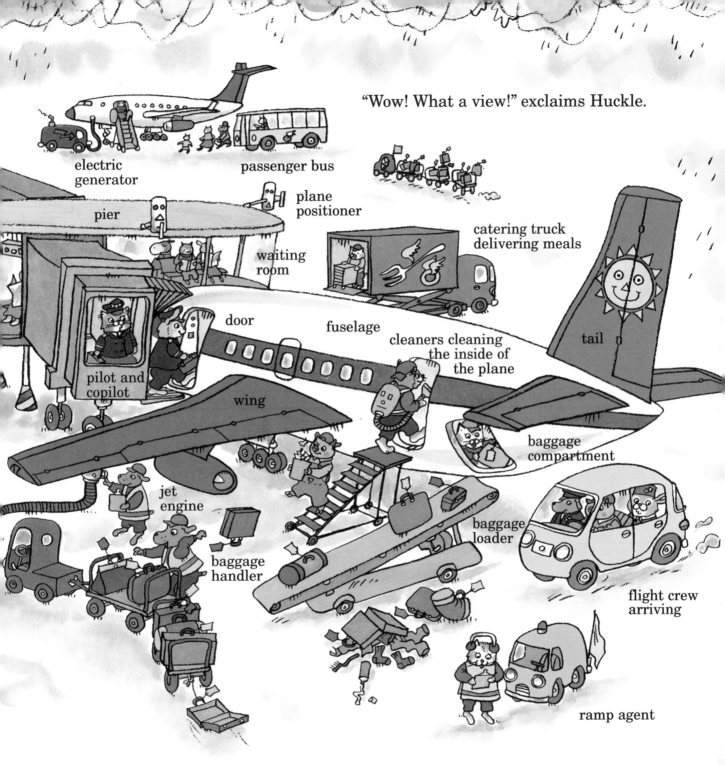

electric generator

passenger bus

"Wow! What a view!" exclaims Huckle.

plane positioner

pier

waiting room

catering truck delivering meals

door

fuselage

cleaners cleaning the inside of the plane

tail

pilot and copilot

wing

baggage compartment

jet engine

baggage loader

baggage handler

flight crew arriving

ramp agent

tractor

Rudolf drives over to the control tower.
Please take care driving up the stairs, Rudolf.

catering kitchen
preparing meals

searchlight

radio antenna

runway

binoculars

ground controller

a taxiing plane heading for the runway

control tower

follow-me car guiding landed airplanes

a pilot studying the weather

weatherman

FOLLOW ME

in winter, snowplows clear the runways and taxiways

"From up here, each plane receives instructions by radio—where to park and when to take off and land," Rudolf explains. "At night and in fog, you can still see every plane on this radar screen."

DON'T STEP ON THE GRASS.

radar antenna

radar screen

"Busy Air Flight One, you're clear for takeoff," says the ground controller into the microphone.

The big plane races down the runway and soars into the sky. *Whooosh!*

Hey! No running on the runway!

wind sock showing the wind's direction

ground controller

"Mr. Von Flugel," says Sally, "you know so much. Can you tell me what that funny-looking thing over there is?"

Just a little to the right!

cargo plane

"Ach! I almost forgot!" cries Rudolf.
He drives across the runway, past a
cargo plane being loaded with freight
containers.

airplane hangars

luggage
trolleys

freight
containers

"These are the hangars,
Sally," says Rudolf. "Inside,
airplanes are parked and
repaired."

"Thank you, Mr. Von Flugel,"
Sally replies. "But what's *that*!?"
she asks, pointing.

"Ach! *This* is my Bratwurst Balloon!" Rudolf says. "Quick! Hop in before you get wet!"

"Look out, everyone!" calls the ground controller. "Here comes the Bratwurst Balloon!"

Soon they are high in the sky.

"Look! There's our house!" says Huckle.
"Mom! Dad! Look up!" he calls.

No, look *out,* Rudolf! Your Bratwurst Balloon is about to burst.

Bump! They all land safely on Huckle's front lawn.

"Well, Rudolf, that was a perfect landing," says Father Cat.

"Thank you, Mr. Von Flugel!" say Huckle, Sally, and Lowly.

"This has been the best afternoon ever!"

Richard Scarry's
A Day at
the Fire Station

"Wonderful!" replies
Chief Smokey.

Drippy and Sticky, the housepainters,
pull up in front of the Busytown fire station.
"We're here to paint the firehouse!"
says Drippy.

"But please don't park your paint truck in front of the firehouse doors," Smokey says. "We firefighters have to be able to drive out at ANY time."

After parking their paint truck out of the way, Drippy and Sticky enter the fire station.

"Wow! What a nifty place!" says Drippy.

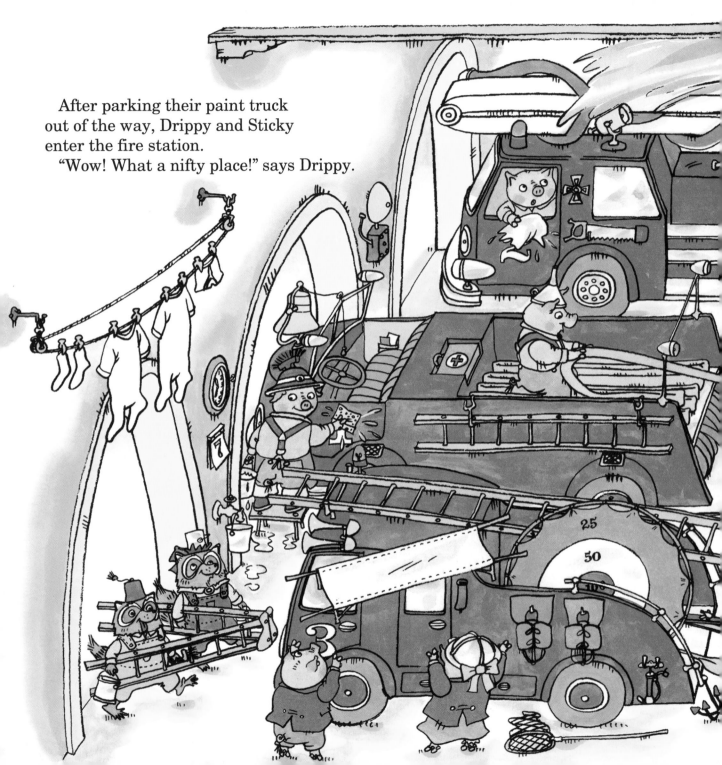

The firefighters are busy cleaning their fire engines.
"We firefighters like to keep our engines nice and clean,
so please be careful not to get any paint on them,"
says Smokey.

"Aye-aye, sir!" replies Sticky.

Drippy covers a fire engine with a big cloth so that it won't get dripped on. Sticky opens the cans of paint.

Drippy begins to paint the firehouse ceiling pink.
Sticky starts to paint the firehouse poles in candy stripes.

Oops! Drippy's cloth seems to have slipped off the fire engine.

"My red fire engine!" shouts Smokey. "It's pink!"

"Don't worry," says Drippy. "We'll have your fire engine cleaned up in no time."

But instead of rubbing off, the wet paint smears in long streaks. What a mess!

RRRINNG! RRRINNG! sounds a loud bell. It's the fire station alarm!

The firefighters sleeping in the dormitory upstairs leap from their beds and slide down the poles to the engines below.

"Oh, no!" shout Drippy and Sticky.
"Oh, no!" shout the firefighters,
covered in candy-stripe paint.

But stained uniforms or no, the brave firefighters jump into their boots, grab their coats and helmets, and charge out of the fire station aboard their red—and pink— fire engines. WWWRRRR! CLANG! CLANG!

"Well," says Drippy, "now that the firefighters are gone, perhaps we can get our painting done."

The firefighters have been called out to a traffic accident. Cecelia's cement mixer bumped into Horace's honey truck and knocked over Farmer Hal's haywagon. What a gooey mess!

Thank goodness for the firefighters! They will have everything cleaned up in no time.

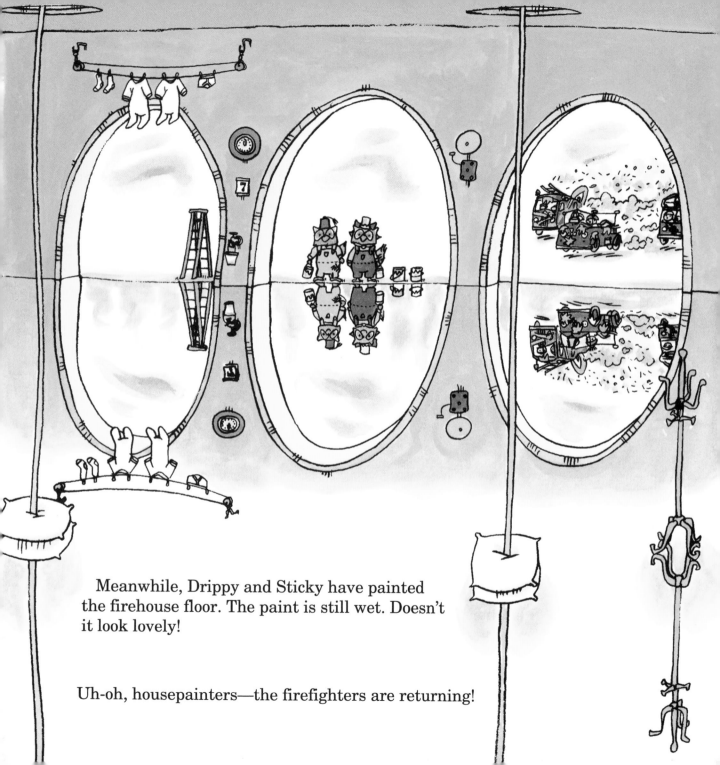

Meanwhile, Drippy and Sticky have painted
the firehouse floor. The paint is still wet. Doesn't
it look lovely!

Uh-oh, housepainters—the firefighters are returning!

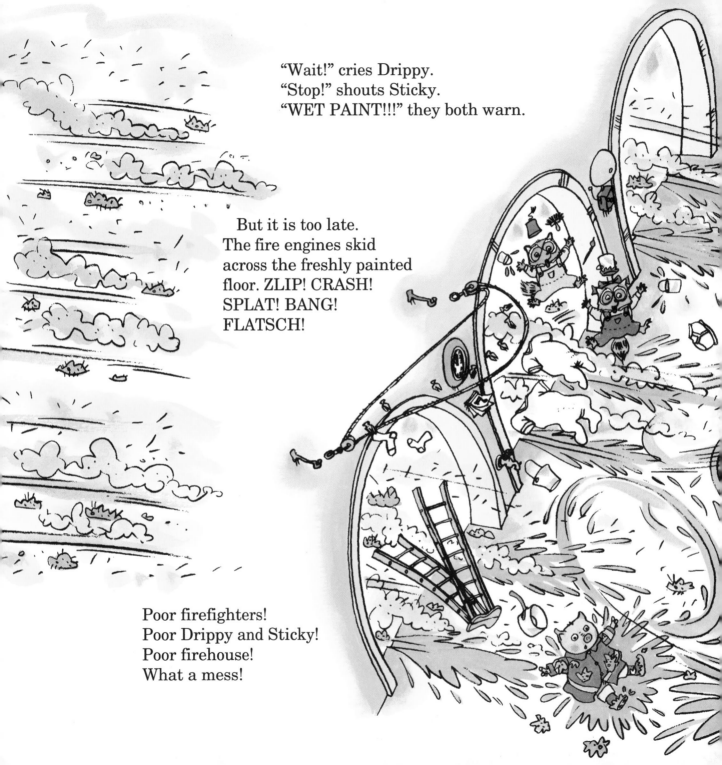

"Wait!" cries Drippy.
"Stop!" shouts Sticky.
"WET PAINT!!!" they both warn.

But it is too late.
The fire engines skid
across the freshly painted
floor. ZLIP! CRASH!
SPLAT! BANG!
FLATSCH!

Poor firefighters!
Poor Drippy and Sticky!
Poor firehouse!
What a mess!

Straw and cement and honey are EVERYWHERE.

Smokey picks up a hose and sprays out the fire station. SWWIIIIIIIIISH! SWWOOOOOSH!

Suddenly, there is another alarm.
This time, it's a fire!

The firefighters throw all their equipment
into the fire engines and are off to the rescue.

Look! It's a fire at Vesuvio's Peppery Pizza Parlor! The firefighters quickly hook up the pumper engine to the fire hydrant and bravely rush inside.

The fire is in the oven! (It's a burnt pizza.)
Hurry, firefighters!
With a spray of water from the hose, the fire is put out.

To thank the firefighters, Vesuvio invites
them all to a big pizza lunch. Isn't he nice?

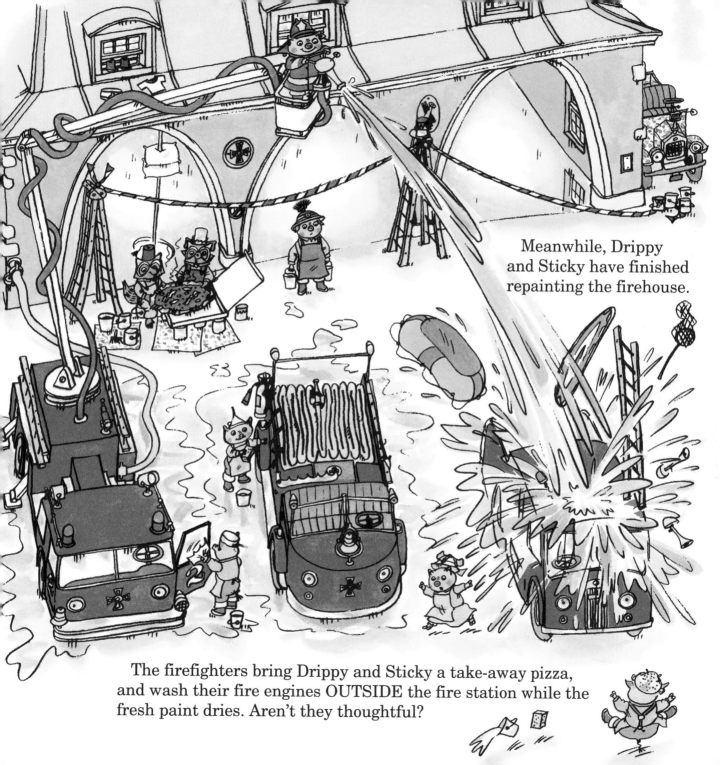

Meanwhile, Drippy and Sticky have finished repainting the firehouse.

The firefighters bring Drippy and Sticky a take-away pizza, and wash their fire engines OUTSIDE the fire station while the fresh paint dries. Aren't they thoughtful?

Just then, Tammy Tapir drives up
in her strawberry jam truck.
"Can anyone please tell me how
to get to the thruway from here?"
Tammy asks the firefighters.

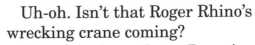

Uh-oh. Isn't that Roger Rhino's
wrecking crane coming?
Hey, slow down there, Roger!

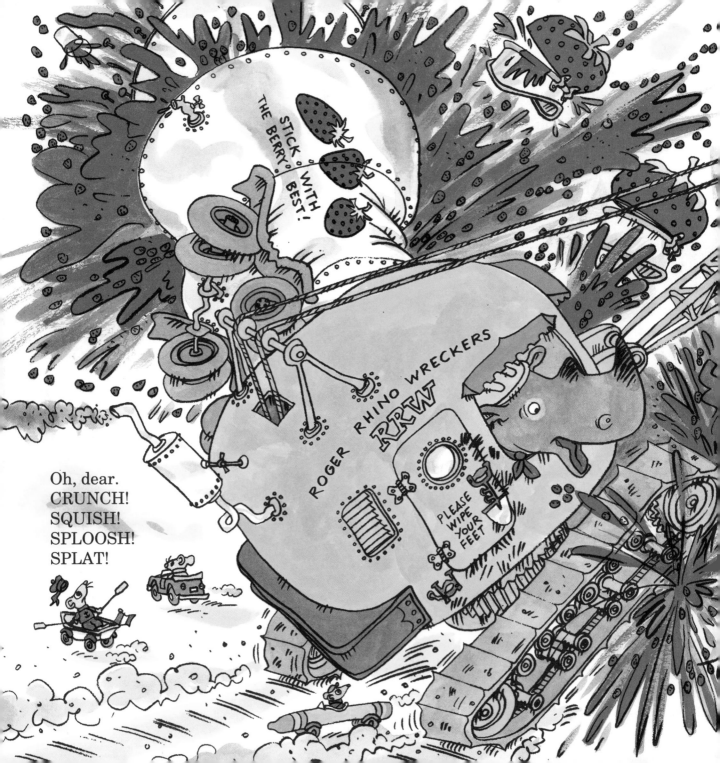

Nice work, Roger!

"Gee, I'm awfully sorry about this," says Roger, apologizing.
"Oh, don't worry," says Smokey with a sigh. "We'll have
this cleaned up in no time. It's all in a firefighter's day
at the fire station."